W9-AYN-173

WELCOME TO
PASSPORT TO READING
A beginning reader's ticket to a brand-new world!

Every book in this program is designed to build read-along and read-alone skills, level by level, through engaging and enriching stories. As the reader turns each page, he or she will become more confident with new vocabulary, sight words, and comprehension.

These PASSPORT TO READING levels will help you choose the perfect book for every reader.

READING TOGETHER
Read short words in simple sentence structures together to begin a reader's journey.

READING OUT LOUD
Encourage developing readers to sound out words in more complex stories with simple vocabulary.

READING INDEPENDENTLY
Newly independent readers gain confidence reading more complex sentences with higher word counts.

READY TO READ MORE
Readers prepare for chapter books with fewer illustrations and longer paragraphs.

This book features sight words from the educator-supported Dolch Sight Words List. This encourages the reader to recognize commonly used vocabulary words, increasing reading speed and fluency.

For more information, please visit passporttoreadingbooks.com.

Enjoy the journey!

TM & © 2014 DC Comics.
TEEN TITANS GO! and all related characters and elements
are trademarks of and © DC Comics.
(s14)

Cover design by Tim Hall

All rights reserved. In accordance with the U.S. Copyright Act of 1976, the scanning, uploading, and electronic sharing of any part of this book without the permission of the publisher is unlawful piracy and theft of the author's intellectual property. If you would like to use material from the book (other than for review purposes), prior written permission must be obtained by contacting the publisher at permissions@hbgusa.com. Thank you for your support of the author's rights.

Little, Brown and Company

Hachette Book Group
1290 Avenue of the Americas, New York, NY 10104
Visit us at lb-kids.com

Little, Brown and Company is a division of Hachette Book Group, Inc.
The Little, Brown name and logo are trademarks of Hachette Book Group, Inc.

The publisher is not responsible for websites (or their content)
that are not owned by the publisher.

First Edition: October 2014

ISBN 978-0-316-33330-6

Library of Congress Control Number: 2014932609

10 9 8 7 6 5 4 3 2 1

CW

Printed in the United States of America

Passport to Reading titles are leveled by independent reviewers applying the standards developed by Irene Fountas and Gay Su Pinnell in *Matching Books to Readers: Using Leveled Books in Guided Reading*, Heinemann, 1999.

MEET THE TEEN TITANS!

Adapted by Lucy Rosen

Based on the episode "Dude, Relax!"
written by Amy Wolfram

LITTLE, BROWN AND COMPANY
New York   Boston

Attention, Teen Titans fans!
Look for these items when you read
this book. Can you spot them all?

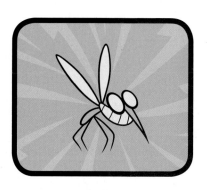

insect

tool

couch

popcorn

The Teen Titans are an awesome bunch.

They combine their superpowers
and become unstoppable!

Cyborg is half-man, half-robot. He escapes danger with his super-strength and powerful armor.

Cyborg's robot parts are great tools.

His jet packs help him fly. His arm cannons help him blast through walls.

And when he gets hungry, he can make snacks!

Beast Boy can change into any animal.
He can shrink down into an insect
or grow into a T. rex.

Whenever he changes shape,
he acts like a new critter.

Beast Boy has a silly side.
You never know what
he will turn into next!

Starfire can fly,
but she does not need a jet pack.
Starfire is an alien
from the planet Tamaran.

Starfire is kind and friendly,
but do not get her mad!
She shoots starbolts from her hands
and starblasts from her eyes.

Starfire has a pet named Silkie.
Silkie does not talk,
but he sure does eat...
anything but tofu.

Beast Boy likes Silkie's style.
He copies it sometimes!

Raven is the most serious of the group.
Her brain is her superpower.
She controls things with her mind
and casts powerful spells.

She can even transport herself
from place to place!

Robin is the Teen Titans' fearless leader.

Robin is different
from the rest of the group.
He cannot fly or change shape.
He cannot move things with his mind.

Robin is a master detective,
an expert pilot,
and a very nimble acrobat.
His friends respect him.
His enemies fear him.

There is one thing that Robin
does not do well.
He does not know how to relax.

"We must always stay alert!" says Robin as he scans his danger detector. "Crime can happen at any moment!"

"Chill out," says Raven.

"I do not know how," Robin replies.

"We will show you," says Cyborg.

"Come with me."

"Try some tinkering," says Cyborg.

He hands Robin a tool.

"Yes, I see," Robin mutters.

"We can take this machine apart
and build something bigger and faster!"

"That is not what I meant," Cyborg says.

But Robin does not hear him.

He is already hard at work.

"Here is something simpler," says Starfire.

"It is a spa mask!"

She spreads green goo all over Robin's face.

"It is made out of pickles and cream cheese," says Starfire.

"Is this not relaxing?"

"No," says Robin.

"But with a few drops of acid, it could make a great weapon."

25

Beast Boy talks to Robin next.

"You have to stop thinking about work,"
Beast Boy says.

"Here. Sit down.

Be one with the couch."

"What do you mean?" Robin asks.

"Watch," says Beast Boy.

Beast Boy leans back.

He closes his eyes

and hums a little song.

Soon he is a part of the furniture!

Robin is confused,
but he is determined.
"I will master oneness
with the couch," he says.

Robin slouches.

He hums.

He starts to drift away.

"Can it be?" the Titans whisper.

"Is Robin really relaxing?"

Just then, a beep goes off.

Robin jumps up from the couch.

"Crime?!" he asks.

"No," says Cyborg.

"Just some popcorn."

The Teen Titans laugh.

"You may not be one with the couch,"
Beast Boy tells Robin,
"but you will always be one of us,
no matter what."
What a great team!